Pass the Jam, Jim!

Pass the Jam, Jim!

Pass the Jam, Jim

Kaye Umansky &
Margaret Chamberlain

RED FOX

Hurry Mabel, lay that table!

Jane, put Wayne back in his pram!

Where's the bread, Fred?
Bread I said, Fred.

Pass the jam, Jim,
Jam, Jim, jam.

Cut the cake,
    Kate.

Pour the tea,
    Lee.

Who wants cheese and who wants ham?

Pass the pot, Dot.
Is it hot, Dot?

Pass the jam, Jim,
Jam, Jim, jam.

Here's the salt, Walt.
Use your spoon, June.

Jill don't spill
And Phil don't cram!

What a mess, Bess,
On your dress, Bess.

Pass the jam, Jim,
Jam, Jim, jam.

Drink your juice,
Bruce.

Slice of pie,
Guy?

Sip your soup up slowly, Sam.

Who's for custard?
Where's the mustard?

Pass the jam, Jim,
Jam, Jim, jam.

Boil the kettle, Gretel.

Bring the butter, Betty.

Charles wants chips and so does Pam.

Thanks a lot, Jim . . .
Oh! You've NOT, Jim!

JIM! YOU'VE EATEN
ALL THE JAM!

A RED FOX BOOK : 9780099185710

First published in Great Britain by Random House Children's Publishers UK 2000
Red Fox edition published 2001

23 25 27 29 30 28 26 24

Text copyright © Kaye Umansky 1992
Illustrations copyright © Margaret Chamberlain 1992
Designed by Rowan Seymour

Red Fox Books are published by Random House Children's Publishers UK,
61-63 Uxbridge Road, London W5 5SA,
a division of The Random House Group Ltd,
Addresses for companies within The Random House Group Limited
can be found at: www.randomhouse.co.uk/offices.htm

THE RANDOM HOUSE GROUP Limited Reg No. 954009
www.randomhousechildrens.co.uk

A CIP catalogue record for this book is available from the British Library.

Printed in Malaysia

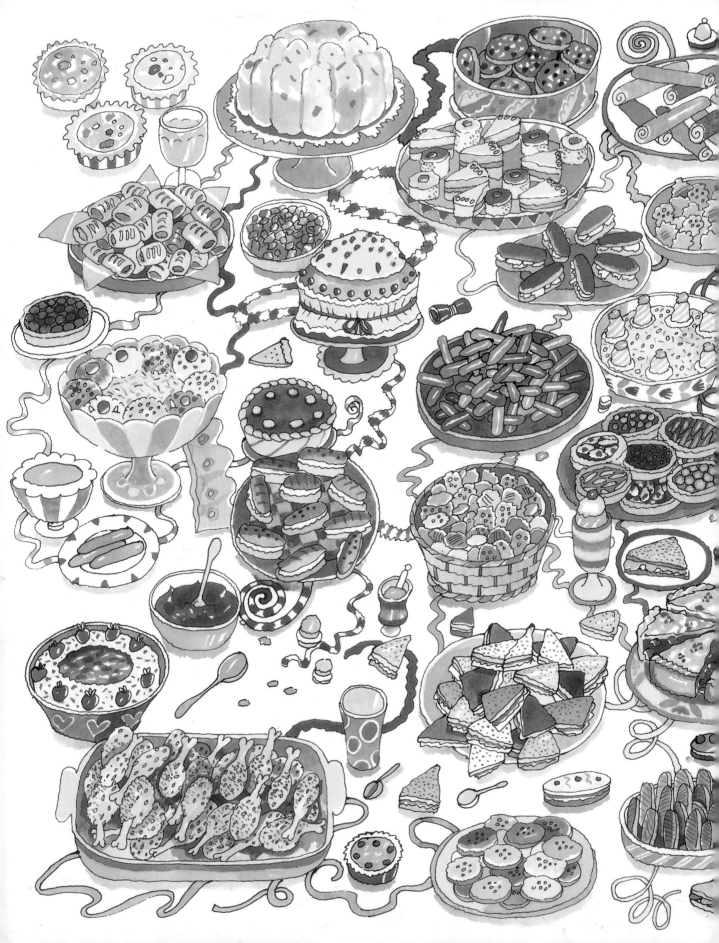